D1467234

A Witch in School

The next morning Marcia found her little squirrel smashed on the floor.

Miss Willow was very sympathetic. She said that no doubt someone had knocked it off accidentally in the excitement the day before. "I'll give you free time today to make another one," she said.

While Marcia was working on a new squirrel, Glenda had to get a dictionary from the cupboard near where Marcia was working.

"There's something funny going on here," Marcia said to her quietly. "Only it's not funny. Somebody in this room is acting like a—like a—*witch*!" Something in Glenda's face had suddenly made her think of the word.

GLENDA GLINKA, WITCH-AT-LARGE

GLENDA GLINKA, WITCH-AT-LARGE

Janice May Udry
Pictures by Marc Simont

■ HarperTrophy®
A Division of HarperCollinsPublishers

Harper Trophy® is a registered trademark
of HarperCollins Publishers Inc.

Originally published as *Glenda*

Glenda Glinka, Witch-At-Large

For information address HarperCollins Children's Books,

a division of HarperCollins Publishers,

10 East 53rd Street, New York, NY 10022.

LC Number: 69-14443

ISBN 0-06-440410-2 (pbk.)

Typography by Steve Scott

First Harper Trophy edition, 1991

Visit us on the World Wide Web!

http://www.harperchildrens.com

✳ CONTENTS

GLENDA GLINKA, WITCH-AT-LARGE

GLENDA GLINKA ✳ 1

Like most witches, Glenda Glinka could change herself into almost anything she wanted to be. She had recently been a rabbit, a bear, a snake, and an umbrella. Changing herself was her favorite amusement—her hobby, you might say. Although Glenda Glinka often used magic, no one had ever caught her using it. She was too clever a witch for that.

But there came a day when she sat drumming her fingers, unable to decide what she would like to be. Nothing she thought of seemed right. A chicken? A peacock? A snail? A fairy godmother? A parrot? A pillow?

No, none of those things. She had already been most of them. Glenda became so restless and fidgety that she took a walk into town.

It happened that she was passing a school just as the children came streaming out at the end of the day.

Glenda watched them. She had turned herself into a shadow because she knew that some children were afraid of witches and she didn't want any yelling that day.

The boys and girls came out the doors, chattering and calling to each other. Some of them got onto school buses. Some of them started walking or running down the street under the bright blue September sky.

Glenda watched the little girls especially. If she had ever been a little girl herself, it was so long ago that she couldn't remember it. She noticed their bright-colored dresses and sweaters and socks.

I wonder what it's like in there—in the school. What do they do all day? What do they talk about?

Glenda watched until the last little girl had run out the door and galloped down the walk and around the corner.

In a little while some of the teachers came out. None of them ran.

But Glenda was still thinking about the little girls. I'll bet that's fun—being a little girl and going to school! I believe I'll try it! That's something I've never been—that I can remember. I'll concentrate on that tonight, and tomorrow I'll be here wearing the prettiest dress of all!

Cackling happily to herself, Glenda the shadow left the tree she had been leaning against and tried skipping down the walk as she had seen some of the little girls skip. No one was around to see that long thin shadow skip by itself around the corner.

The New Girl ✷ 2

The next morning Glenda was one of the first children at school. She looked like almost any other little schoolgirl. She had soft brown hair and a sweet little face. But she was certainly wearing the prettiest dress in the school.

Glenda could feel the other little girls looking at the dress and admiring it. She liked that. She hoped they envied it.

She had worked almost all night on that dress. She had wanted to be sure her dress was prettier than any other dress in the school.

Finally, one little girl came up to her. "Are

you a new girl?" she asked. "I like your dress. It's so pretty. Did your mother make it?"

Glenda noticed that the little girl's dress was definitely not new. She thought, I bet she wishes she had a dress like mine. She almost told her that she had made the dress herself. No, I mustn't say that! Little girls can't make dresses like this. I'll have to say my mother made it. I've got to remember that I am a little girl with a mother now. I'll have to be careful. Being a little girl will be trickier than being a rabbit or a chicken!

She smiled sweetly. "Yes, I'm a new girl. My name is Glenda. My mother made my new dress."

Another girl joined the first one. "Your mother sure can sew! My name is Marcia. She's Karen. Where do you live?"

Where do I live? thought Glenda nervously. Drat! I should have thought all these things out first. Where shall I say I live?

"Down the street. Around the corner. Not far from here," she mumbled.

Glenda really lived at the edge of town in a very old farmhouse with broken windows. But she didn't think she should tell Marcia and Karen that.

"Why didn't your mother come with you the first day?" asked Marcia curiously. "Mothers usually come to a new school the first day."

Being so unfamiliar with thinking about mothers, Glenda didn't know what to answer. I guess I should have said I was an orphan, she thought. Too late now.

Karen helped her out. "Maybe her mother works," she said.

"That's right," said Glenda quickly. "My mother works."

Drawn by the lovely dress and the new face, other little girls kept coming up to Glenda.

"What's her name? That's the prettiest dress I ever saw!" they said, pushing to get a better look. "What grade is she in?"

Glenda smoothed her hair. The other little

girls admired her already. When the bell rang, she held her head up, smiled sweetly, and passed into the school, surrounded by a circle of curious, admiring little girls.

I guess I'm doing all right, Glenda thought to herself. I am really a clever witch!

GLENDA'S FLOWERS ✳ 3

Glenda's teacher, Miss Willow, didn't say anything about her beautiful dress, so the next day Glenda brought her a glorious bouquet of flowers.

"She'll have to notice *this*!" said Glenda smugly as she swooped down the hill toward school. "My bouquet will make that other bouquet on the teacher's desk look like weeds."

"Oh, Glenda! Those beautiful flowers!" gasped the girls when they saw her on the playground.

"Miss Willow will love those," said Karen, her gentle blue eyes filled with admiration.

The flowers on Miss Willow's desk from the day before were from Karen. They were the last three small zinnias from Karen's summer flower bed. Compared with Glenda's picture-book bouquet, they did indeed look like weeds.

"Why, thank you, Glenda!" said Miss Willow when Glenda gave her the flowers. "I don't know what to say! I'll take these to my mother tonight. She is not very well, and I am sure they will give her a lot of pleasure."

Glenda went to her desk, feeling very self-satisfied. She thought, No other pupil ever gave flowers *that* beautiful.

All morning the flowers on Miss Willow's desk almost seemed to fill the room. They glowed and sparkled so much that the children and even Miss Willow could scarcely take their eyes off them.

After lunch, Miss Willow began passing out large sheets of the best art paper. She asked one of the boys, Tom, to pass out the paints.

"I hadn't intended to have a painting lesson today," she said. "But I decided we shouldn't pass up this chance to paint Glenda's lovely flowers."

Wait till they see *my* picture, thought Glenda, digging vigorously into a paintpot. But she soon found that painting was not so easy.

If only I dared use magic, thought Glenda, I'd make a picture they would never forget. But she knew she couldn't cast a spell in the classroom, or she'd give herself away as a witch.

When they were finished and Miss Willow had hung all the pictures up to dry, it was easy to see who had painted the best one. It was certainly not Glenda. In fact, Glenda's was easily the poorest painting in the room.

"Alice, you've done a beautiful painting," said Miss Willow.

Glenda turned around and glared at Alice. I'd like to change her into a pig, she thought angrily.

But since Glenda wanted everyone to believe she was a typical schoolgirl, she couldn't allow herself to change anybody into anything. It was very frustrating.

"Glenda, will you collect the paintbrushes for us, please? Everyone clean up now," said Miss Willow.

Glenda began going up and down the aisles, grabbing the brushes off the desks. When she came to Alice, she seemed to trip. Falling sideways, she knocked the jars of paint off the desk so that Alice's dress was spattered and splotched with paint.

"Oh, dear!" said Glenda, but she was grinning.

All the children turned around and gasped. What a mess!

"Quick, Glenda! Go get the paper towels!" said Miss Willow. "Children, back in your seats. We simply must be very careful when we use the paints!"

Glenda skipped down the hall for paper towels.

Poor Alice stood dripping, dabbing at her ruined dress with a handkerchief. But up in front of the room her lovely picture was unspoiled delight.

The Leaf Notebooks ✳ 4

Miss Willow wanted all of the children to make a leaf collection by pressing different leaves under heavy books and then taping them into a notebook and labeling them.

On the day that the leaf notebooks were due, Glenda marched up the walk to school, carrying the thickest notebook of all.

I'll bet no one has more leaves than I have! she thought. And she was right.

"Where on earth did you find so many?" asked Betsy when Glenda opened her book for the other girls to see.

"Did you have your brother or somebody help you find them?" asked Marcia.

"I did it all myself," said Glenda.

"You'll certainly get an A, Glenda," said Karen. "I haven't got half that many."

Alice had brought a jump rope to school, so the girls put their leaf notebooks on a bench and took turns jumping and chanting jump-rope songs.

Glenda wasn't very good at jumping rope, so she didn't really want to play.

"Let's not jump rope," she said. "It's too hot."

"Oh, come on, Glenda. It's not hot," said Marcia.

Reluctantly she joined them.

The girls began with *Teddy Bear*. "Teddy Bear, Teddy Bear, turn around; Teddy Bear, Teddy Bear, touch the ground; Teddy Bear, Teddy Bear, go upstairs . . ."

When Glenda's turn to jump came, she missed on the fifth jump. She stamped down on the rope impatiently. "The wind blew the rope. That's what made me miss," she said.

She saw Marcia wink at Karen and got

furious. In a huff, she sat down next to the leaf notebooks. She wished the bell would hurry up and ring. Marcia was jumping, and she had already reached eighty-nine without stopping or missing.

Glenda looked sideways at the notebooks. Marcia's was on top.

Just then some of the boys came galloping over to tease the girls. They often did this because jumping rope really looked like fun to the boys, but they would never admit it. The next best thing to joining the girls was trying to spoil their jumping.

"Look at the little girls jumping their little rope!" jeered John.

"Jumpy, jumpy, jump, jump!" teased Fred.

The girls pretended to ignore them. Marcia went on jumping.

Finally Tom grabbed at the rope, making Marcia miss.

"You made me miss, Tom Taylor! You pest!" She tried to hit him, but Tom danced

out of reach, laughing. All the girls turned on the boys for spoiling their game.

No one was paying any attention to Glenda.

Suddenly Glenda's elbow jerked out sharply, and Marcia's notebook flew into the air as if thrown and came sprawling down open onto the ground. The wind fluttered some of the pages while it was in the air, causing some of the leaves to come untaped and fly away.

The school bell rang.

The boys departed, and the girls hurried to get their notebooks.

"My notebook!" cried Marcia, rushing to pick it up.

"It was the wind," said Glenda.

"I'll bet one of those boys did it," said Marcia, brushing dirt from the pages. "Some of the leaves are gone! It's practically ruined!"

"You should have taped them in better," said Glenda.

The Princess Part ✳ 5

"Karen told me she hoped Miss Willow wouldn't choose you to be the princess in the play because she thought you wouldn't make a good princess at all," Glenda told Marcia at recess one day.

"Did she really say that?" demanded Marcia.

"Yes, she did. Of course, she told me not to tell you. But I thought you'd want to know what she really thinks of you," said Glenda calmly.

"Well, I'd like to know what makes Karen think she is such a good judge of who could be a princess and who couldn't. She would certainly be the worst one in the room to be picked for princess!"

"Marcia told me she hoped Miss Willow wouldn't choose you to be the princess because she thought you would be the worst one in the school," Glenda told Karen while they were standing in the cafeteria line.

"Did she really say that?" asked Karen.

"Yes, she did. Of course, she told me not to tell you. But I thought you'd want to know," said Glenda.

"Well, thank you for telling me!" said Karen angrily, with tears in her eyes.

Glenda was delighted when Karen and Marcia stopped speaking to each other.

Miss Willow was having everyone in the room try out for the different parts of a fairy-tale play. It became clear to Miss Willow and the other children that Karen and Marcia especially were trying to outdo each other when they read for the princess part.

Instead of talking together before school in the mornings now, the girls stood in two little groups—Marcia in one and Karen in the other. Often one of the girls didn't get to school until the bell was ringing. When Miss Willow took the class out for relay races, Karen and Marcia were never on the same team. They never sat together at a table in the cafeteria anymore.

Some of the girls said they hoped Karen would be princess, and some of them said they hoped that Marcia would be. Glenda didn't say anything. She hoped to be princess herself.

Finally Miss Willow said, "I am sorry to take so long in choosing the cast for the play, boys and girls. You've been very patient. You all read so well I can't make up my mind. I've decided to let the class choose by secret ballot."

Each child wrote his choices for the different parts on small pieces of paper and folded them. Fred walked down the aisles with an empty box, and each child put his votes into the box.

Then Miss Willow opened the papers. After reading and counting the votes, she wrote the names of the actors and actresses on the blackboard.

Karen and Marcia had tied for the part of princess. Even though Glenda had voted for herself, the other two girls still had more votes.

Karen raised her hand. She was very pale. "I don't feel well, Miss Willow. May I be excused?"

"Certainly," said Miss Willow. "Go right down to the nurse, Karen." Karen left the room.

The next day Betsy reported that Karen had chicken pox. Three days later Alice reported that Marcia wasn't at school because she also had chicken pox.

Miss Willow decided to go ahead with the play. Glenda was chosen princess because she had received the most votes after Karen and Marcia.

Glenda did not get chicken pox.

Glenda was certain that she knew exactly how this princess should act and talk. She also thought she knew how all the other parts should be played, and she told the other girls and boys so as often as Miss Willow would permit.

Glenda spoke all her lines good and loud. And somehow or other, most of the time she was on the stage, she was standing in front of someone else. After the play the other girls talked for days about the fantastic princess costume Glenda wore.

BRING-A-PET WEEK ✳ 6

When the class came to the chapter in the science book on animal life, Miss Willow said that they could each bring an example of animal life from home—if it was in a small box or cage.

"We will call this Bring-a-Pet Week. You should only bring a creature that you can easily carry to and from school without any help," said Miss Willow. "Be sure to bring food for your pets."

Into Miss Willow's room that week came jars of grasshoppers, frogs, and turtles—and one garter snake. A hamster, a mouse, a kitten, and a rabbit also arrived—each in its own box.

"I'm going to bring my talking crow," announced Glenda.

Kazbo made a terrible fuss about getting into a cage.

Glenda had owned him for many years, but he had never been inside a cage in his life.

"What's *that*?" he yelled when Glenda brought it out and dusted it off.

"You know what it is," said Glenda. "Don't pretend you don't know what a cage is. You're going to school with me tomorrow, because nobody else has a talking pet."

"School! Me?" cried the crow. "School with all those what-do-you-call-'ems?"

"Do you mean children?" said Glenda. "Well, of course there will be children there, but they won't hurt you."

"I don't trust 'em," said Kazbo, hunching up his shoulders. "Never did."

He spied the cat going out the door to hunt for mice.

"Why don't you take Zachary? Why me? He would fit into that what-cha-ma-call-it—cage—just as well as I would."

"No, I don't want to take a cat. There's already a kitten in the room. I want something unusual. And that's you. Come on now, just go in the little door. It's a nice comfortable cage, and here's some corn."

"No!" screeched Kazbo. "I'll never go in there. Never!"

Glenda stamped her foot. "Then you're going to get awfully hungry, because your dinner is in there and you'll have to go into the cage to get it!" And she put a cup of corn, which the crow loved, inside the cage.

"I'll starve first!" shouted Kazbo. But he eyed the corn hungrily.

In the morning, Kazbo still had not gone into the cage to eat.

"I'm weak from hunger," he wailed. "I'm dying."

"Go into the cage then," said Glenda.

"Hurry up! I'm almost late for school."

Slowly, sorrowfully, like a man walking to the gallows, Kazbo climbed into the cage.

Glenda snapped the door shut. "Now we're ready," she crooned.

Kazbo gobbled corn all the way to school and never said a word.

"Be nice, and don't say anything rude in the classroom," said Glenda as they neared the playground.

"Don't worry," said Kazbo, popping the last kernel of corn into his beak. "I won't say anything rude, because I'm not going to say anything at all. I am not going to say one word!" He chortled triumphantly.

"You've got to talk," said Glenda. "If you don't say anything, you'll just be a plain old crow!"

"I don't care if those what-do-you-call-'ems don't know I can talk. I don't want them to know."

"But I told them that you talk!" wailed Glenda. "You've got to talk."

"No, I don't," said Kazbo. "They'll think I'm a clam."

And he tucked his head under his wing. With his stomach full of corn, he was soon sound asleep.

"Wake up!" said Glenda, banging on the bars of the cage.

Kazbo never stirred.

"Wake up!" shouted Glenda, clomping the cage on the sidewalk. But it was no use. The crow never moved a feather.

True to his word, Kazbo never spoke a word in Miss Willow's class. In fact, he barely seemed alive except when he was eating. Glenda had to feed him because Miss Willow made sure that all the visiting pets were being well cared for.

"Is he sick?" asked Fred. "He barely moves."

"I thought you said he could talk," said John. "When is he going to start?"

"He does talk," muttered Glenda, "when

he wants to."

"Can't you make him?" asked Tom.

"Not here," said Glenda.

"I'll bet he can't talk," said Fred. "He's just a plain old crow."

Friday after school, Glenda took Kazbo home in his cage and banged him down. She opened the door of the cage.

"I hope you're satisfied," she said.

"Yes, indeed," said Kazbo. "I enjoyed my visit to Miss Willow's class. Those little what-do-you-call-'ems weren't bad at all. I really enjoyed listening to the school lessons. I learned quite a bit. But I could hardly keep from laughing sometimes when I heard you talking so sweetly to the teacher. By the way, you can't draw very well, can you? Not like that girl Alice."

"EEEEEK!" he yelled as he flew up onto a rafter. Glenda had thrown the cage at him. "Temper, temper, little girl!" he mocked.

The P.T.A. Cookies ✳ 7

The next week Miss Willow's class was chosen to supply the cookies for P.T.A. night. The mother of each child in Miss Willow's class received a note asking her to make cookies.

"Don't forget to bring your P.T.A. cookies tomorrow," reminded Miss Willow as the last bell of the day rang.

What are P.T.A. cookies? wondered Glenda as she trotted home. I know how to make cookies, but will they be the right kind for P.T.A. cookies?

"Let's play cards," said Kazbo as soon as she put her books down. "It's been a boring rainy day. I almost wish I'd been at school with you."

"Can't play cards," said Glenda, getting out a cauldron. "I've got to make P.T.A. cookies. Do you know what they're like?"

Kazbo cocked his head. "P.T.A. cookies? Never heard of them. But if we knew what the *P*, *T*, and *A* stood for, maybe it would help."

Kazbo knocked the dictionary off the shelf and began to flip pages with his sharp yellow beak. "Here we are," he murmured, "abbreviations."

He walked down the P page. "*P.T.* means Pacific Time. That's not it. Here—*P.T.A.*, Parent-Teachers' Association. That's it. You've got to make some Parent-Teachers' Association cookies," he said, shutting the book as if that settled it.

"I don't know what kind that is either," said Glenda. "Oh, well, here goes. I'll just have to make the kind I usually make and hope they will be all right."

"What color are you going to make them?" asked Kazbo.

Glenda thought. "I haven't made purple ones for a long time. How about two batches, one purple and one green?"

"That ought to do it," said Kazbo. "Are you going to put in those little crunchy beetles this time?"

"Of course," said Glenda. "I want these to be the best P.T.A. cookies there!"

Glenda mixed and stirred and baked until quite late. When she had finished, Kazbo sampled one. "Delicious!" he declared. "Really superb."

"They ought to be good," said Glenda. "I did my best. My persimmon tree was loaded this year. I put in a lot of green-persimmon pulp, as well as the beetles. That gives them zip."

"I have to say that you make the best cookies I ever ate," said Kazbo.

"Thank you," said Glenda. Kazbo rarely paid anyone a compliment, so she felt

confident that the cookies must be very good. She went to bed, tired but content.

"How many cookies did your mother make?" asked Betsy when she met Glenda at the corner. Betsy was carrying a shoebox full of cookies. Glenda was barely able to carry two boxes about the size of suit boxes. One box was full of green cookies, and the other box was full of purple ones.

"What kind are they?" asked Betsy.

"They're P.T.A. cookies, of course!" said Glenda.

The morning after the P.T.A. meeting some of the parents asked their children whose mother had sent the little green and purple cookies.

"Why do you want to know?" asked the children.

"Oh, no reason really," their parents answered hastily. "No reason."

✴   ✴   ✴

The janitor was puzzled to find little purple and green cookies all over the meeting room—each with just one bite gone.

"That's funny," he said, scooping them up. "Nobody seemed to like these." He sniffed one. He took a small bite. *"Uch!"* he said and quickly swept them up into the trash. But Glenda never knew.

THE MAP OF AFRICA ✳ 8

The next day Miss Willow told the class to study the map of Africa in their geography books. Then she told them to close their books and draw the map freehand, without looking at the book. While they were working, Miss Willow was called out of the room for a few minutes.

At the end of the period, Miss Willow collected the maps. After she looked through them, she held up Glenda's.

"This is a very good map, Glenda. Yours is the most accurate."

"But Miss Willow—" said Marcia without raising her hand.

Miss Willow frowned. "Did you wish to say something, Marcia? I don't believe you raised your hand."

"Excuse me," mumbled Marcia.

"All right, Marcia," said Miss Willow. "What did you wish to say?"

"Nothing," said Marcia. "I'm sorry, Miss Willow."

Marcia was the only one in the room who had seen Glenda open her book and trace the map of Africa.

After school, Marcia caught up with Glenda at the corner of the schoolyard.

"I saw you trace the map," Marcia told her. "That wasn't fair, you know."

Glenda stared at Marcia. She stamped her feet. Then she flew into a rage.

"Shut up and mind your own business!" she shouted. "You did not see me trace it! I wish I could change you into a toad!" Then she turned and ran from the schoolyard so fast that Marcia could only stare in amazement.

"What a temper!" said Marcia in awe. "I wonder if they let her act like that at home."

She turned and walked thoughtfully the other way, toward her own home. I know I saw her trace that map. I wonder why Miss Willow couldn't see that it was traced.

Glenda was still furious at Marcia the next day.

Being very careful that no one saw her do it, she put a spider in Marcia's hair. Spiders didn't frighten Glenda, but she knew that most girls nearly flew apart when they saw even a small one.

Sure enough, when Alice, who sat behind Marcia, saw it she screamed with such horror that Miss Willow broke her chalk.

"SPIDER!" she shrieked.

All the other girls got out of their seats, squealing and pressing their backs to the wall while poor Marcia batted her head and shook her hair. When the spider fell to the floor, Glenda stepped on it.

"Thank you, Glenda," said Miss Willow. "Back to your seats, girls."

Soon after that, Marcia found that every colored pencil in her new set had been broken in half.

And at the end of the day when she went to get her sweater, she found that it was tied in three hard knots.

"Well, for heaven's sake, look at your sweater!" said Glenda. "I'll bet one of the boys did that. Here, have some candy."

"No, thank you," said Marcia, tugging at the knots.

Glenda popped a piece of candy into her mouth and walked calmly down the hall.

Marcia looked after her suspiciously.

It was a good thing Marcia didn't take the candy. Glenda was eating Atomic Fireballs—the hottest candy at the candy store. Glenda actually enjoyed them, but no one else ever ate one except on a dare.

DOROTHY ✳ 9

"The new girl—that Dorothy—talks funny, doesn't she?" said Glenda to Karen.

"She moved here from out west some where. Was it Montana?" said Karen.

"Well, she sounds dumb. She talks like a dope," said Glenda. "Here she comes now. She's too friendly."

The new girl came up to them eagerly. "Howdy, Karen. Howdy, Glenda. It's a pretty day, sure enough. Where I used to live it might be snowin' by now."

"I bet you used to live out in the sticks— way out in cow country," said Glenda.

"I did," said Dorothy. "I went to a little country school in the mountains. We usually wore blue jeans to school—hardly ever dresses like here."

"That *was* the sticks. Are you wearing your brother's shoes?" asked Glenda, noticing the heavy oxfords that Dorothy wore.

Dorothy's face flushed. "No, they're not my brother's. It's the kind of shoes I wore for school back home."

"How come you wear the same jumper every day?" asked Glenda.

Before Dorothy could answer, Marcia and some of the other girls came over.

"Hi, Karen, Glenda," said Marcia. "Hi, Dorothy. How do you like it here by now?"

Dorothy turned gratefully to Marcia. "I like it pretty well so far. Can I sit by you in the cafeteria today, Marcia?"

"Sure," said Marcia.

"You can sit anywhere. It's a free country," said Glenda. "Did they have a cafeteria in your other school?"

"No, they didn't," said Dorothy. "We all took our lunch in a pail."

"In a pail? Do you mean you took your lunch in a *bucket*? Was it soup?" asked Glenda, pretending great surprise. She looked to see if the others were laughing—but Marcia was frowning. The others listened as if almost hypnotized.

"N-n-o," stammered Dorothy. "I mean a lunch box. We called them dinner pails back there."

"Well, did you have electricity?" asked Glenda.

"Oh, yes," laughed Dorothy. "We got that when I was about five years old."

"I'll bet the mountains are beautiful," said Marcia.

"They used to call Montana the Land of the Shining Mountains," said Dorothy. "We lived in the Crazy Mountains."

"The *Crazy Mountains*? Did you really? Was the name of your school the Crazy School?" asked Glenda. She laughed loudly.

"What if it *was* called the Crazy School?" said Marcia. "What if it did have a funny name?"

"It was just called Sweet Grass School," said Dorothy in a low voice. "That was the name of the county it was in."

"Well, thank goodness," said Glenda in mock relief.

The bell rang.

"Why are you being so mean to her?" asked Marcia as they moved down the hall with all the other chattering children.

"Mean?" said Glenda. "I'm not being mean. I'm just teasing her a little bit. I hope she can take a joke!"

GLENDA'S CLUB ✳ 10

"I am forming a club," announced Glenda.

"May I be in it?" asked Karen.

"Yes," said Glenda. "You are invited to join, Karen. You are on my list."

"Am I on your list?" asked Betsy.

"Yes, Betsy, you are on my list too."

"What kind of club?" asked Marcia.

"I haven't exactly decided yet," said Glenda. "First I'm deciding who is going to be in it, and then we'll have a meeting to decide what kind of club it's going to be."

"Will it be for boys and girls or just for girls?" asked Marcia.

"It's a girls' club," said Glenda. "It's strictly for the best girls in Miss Willow's class. No one can be in it unless I invite them."

"What do you mean by best girls?" asked Marcia.

Glenda ignored this question.

By the next day every girl in Miss Willow's class had been invited to join Glenda's club except Marcia and Dorothy.

Some of them said they would join, and some said they would have to ask their mothers first.

"My mother will want to know what kind of club it is," said Alice.

"A club has to have a purpose," said one of the other girls.

"No, it doesn't," said Glenda. "But any way, sometimes the purpose of the club is a secret."

"The purpose of the club is never a secret to the members, is it?" asked Karen.

"Stop worrying about the purpose!" said

Glenda. "The club will be fun. We'll do things."

"Let me see the list," said Betsy. "Which girls are in the club?"

"Almost all the girls in Miss Willow's class are going to be in it," said Glenda.

"Well, who isn't in it then?"

"Actually, only two girls don't qualify," said Glenda.

"Who are they?" persisted Betsy.

"Everybody can be in the club except Marcia and Dorothy," said Glenda.

"Why can't they be in it?" asked Alice.

"Dorothy is too new," said Glenda, "and Marcia is too bossy."

Marcia arrived at the edge of the group in time to hear the last remarks.

She laughed. "I know what kind of club this is," she said, "even if Glenda doesn't."

"What kind?" asked Karen.

"It's a club against somebody," said Marcia. "I even know the name of the club."

"What is the name of it?" asked Betsy.

"It's the A.M.A.D. Club," said Marcia. "The Against-Marcia-and-Dorothy Club."

She walked away, and the girls looked after her uneasily.

"Don't pay any attention to her," said Glenda. "She's just jealous."

"Maybe," said Alice. "All the same, I don't think I want to join it. Thank you anyway for inviting me, Glenda."

"I don't really have time to join a club right now," said Betsy. "I have to practice piano every afternoon now, or my parents won't get me a parakeet."

In the end, all the girls turned down membership in Glenda's club.

Oh, well, it would have been a boring club with those girls in it anyway, thought Glenda on her way home. But that Marcia! She is the most jealous creature I've ever met! I wonder if they let her act like that at home.

T~HE~ F~IRE~ A~LARM~ ✳ 11

All the leaves were gone from the trees, and the days grew colder. The children began wearing their winter coats, and the janitor fired up the school furnace. One Friday afternoon Miss Willow said that it was time to begin making Christmas presents. She brought out a large bag of clay for them to make paperweight animals.

"This is very successful," said Miss Willow after they had been working for a while. "This is a very good lifelike squirrel, Marcia."

"Thank you," murmured Marcia, taking back her successful squirrel after Miss

Willow had held it up for the class to see.

Glenda glared at the squirrel. She had tried to make a cat, but it looked more like a pickle with little pointed ears. She knew that at home she could have made a perfect little clay animal by using magic. Glenda had depended on magic all her life.

I wish Marcia's squirrel would crack, thought Glenda. I wish it would fall apart.

On Monday, after Miss Willow's class had finished painting the clay animals, they put them on the long shelf under the windows to dry. Marcia's squirrel and Glenda's cat were side by side.

Miss Willow gave a note to Glenda and asked her to take it to the principal's office.

While she was gone the fire alarm began to ring.

"FIRE!" someone shouted down the hall.

Some of the girls squealed. The boys jumped out of their seats to look out the windows and the door.

"Be calm, children." said Miss Willow.

"Remember our fire-drill instructions. John, you are fire-drill captain."

All up and down the hall, doors were opened and children marched down the halls. Miss Willow's children formed a line behind John and pressed against each other. The fire alarm continued to clang loudly.

Miss Willow counted the children as they filed out the door, stepping on each other's heels.

Glenda appeared around the corner.

"Oh, there you are," said Miss Willow. "Get in line quickly, Glenda."

"I forgot something," Glenda murmured and dashed into the room.

"Glenda!" shouted Miss Willow.

Glenda reappeared with her coat.

"We never stop for coats," said Miss Willow. "Hurry, Glenda!"

Glenda ran to catch up with the end of her line.

The children were very excited to see that

the fire truck was really there.

"It must be a real fire! It's not just a fire drill!" someone shouted.

The firemen went into the school while all the children and teachers shivered in the cold air.

"Who set off the alarm?"

"Where's the smoke?"

No one knew who had set off the alarm beside the door to the principal's office, and there was no sign of smoke.

Finally, after everyone was blue with cold, one of the firemen came and said that there was no fire.

"It's a false alarm," he said. "You may all go back to your classrooms."

Everyone was so cold, they were in just as much of a hurry to go back in as they had been to get out. All except Glenda, who was smugly wearing her coat.

It was the end of the day, so the children put away their books and went home, talking about the false alarm and what the principal

would do if she ever found out who had done it.

It wasn't until the next morning that Marcia found her little squirrel smashed on the floor.

Miss Willow was very sympathetic. She said that no doubt someone had knocked it off accidentally in the excitement the day before. "I'll give you free time today to make another one," she said.

While Marcia was working on a new squirrel, Glenda had to get a dictionary from the cupboard near where Marcia was working.

"There's something funny going on around here," Marcia said to her quietly. "Only it's not funny. Somebody in this room is acting like a—like a—*witch*!" Something in Glenda's face had suddenly made her think of the word.

Glenda dropped the dictionary with a loud bang. "Shut up," she said to Marcia under her breath as she bent to pick up the book.

"I won't shut up," said Marcia. "And from now on I'll be watching you all the time. I even bet you're the one who caused the false alarm."

Glenda gave her a mixed look of hate and fear and returned to her seat. "She spoils everything," Glenda fumed.

She was even more furious when she saw Karen stop beside Marcia as she worked. They hadn't really been friends since the time when they had both wanted to be the princess in the play.

"It's a shame your squirrel was broken," Karen said. "It was awfully good."

"Thanks," said Marcia warmly. "Your polar bear is good too."

"Can you go to the show with me tomorrow afternoon?" asked Karen.

"I think so," said Marcia. "I'll ask. Let's invite Dorothy too. OK?"

"Sure," said Karen.

Snow ✳ 12

"Well, Kazbo, I think it's been pretty successful," said Glenda.

"What?" Kazbo asked absent-mindedly. He was gazing out the window at the first snowfall of the year.

"My impersonation of a schoolgirl, of course," said Glenda. "I'm just like the others."

"Are you?" said Kazbo. "It's snowing."

"Oh, drat," said Glenda, storming to the window. "I hate snow. It's so white and cold and wet. *Ugh!*"

"It comes down every year around here," observed Kazbo.

"It's funny—the others like snow," said Glenda.

"The other whats?"

"The other girls, stupid!" said Glenda.

"Oh," Kazbo chuckled. "I thought you meant the other witches."

"There's maybe only one thing I hate more than snow," said Glenda.

"What's that?" asked Kazbo.

"Tests," said Glenda. "Miss Willow is always giving tests lately. She gives them, and we take them."

"What are the tests for?" asked Kazbo.

"For grades."

"What are the grades for?"

"To find out who is best."

"Best at what?"

"Best at getting good grades."

"Oh," said Kazbo, cracking corn thoughtfully.

There was a small silence while Glenda gazed out at the swirling snowflakes and Kazbo munched.

"Are you the best?" asked Kazbo.

"Of course I am!" said Glenda, turning from the window angrily. "What kind of a stupid question is that?"

"Don't be so touchy," said Kazbo. "I just asked. How about a change now that it's getting cold and snowing, since you're really tired of taking tests. After all, you didn't intend to go on being a schoolgirl forever, did you?"

"No," said Glenda. "Someday I think I'll be a teacher instead."

"But first why don't we go south for a while?" suggested Kazbo. "Or how about a little vacation in Bermuda?" He began rummaging through some travel folders. "Remember what a good time we had in Hawaii last year?"

Glenda grinned and poked up the fire.

"Let's start packing. We'll leave tomorrow," she said.

"Righto," agreed Kazbo, putting on his sunglasses and hopping along the window sill. "Good-bye, mufflers, snow, and tests!"

"And good-bye, Marcia," said Glenda.

"She wouldn't mind her own business."

"Do you think she suspected something?" asked Kazbo.

"Of course not!" said Glenda. "I'm an actress. When I disguise myself, nobody ever catches on. I'm a clever witch."

"You are!" agreed Kazbo.

"In the spring when we get back, I'll go to school as Miss Glinka, a new substitute teacher. That will be the best yet!" said Glenda happily. "I can be anything I want to be."

"But you'll always be a witch at heart, Glenda," said Kazbo.

"Why, thank you, Kazbo!" grinned Glenda. "You're a clever crow!"

Check Out These Trophy Chapter Books:

The Sam and Robert Bamford Books • Levy
Dracula Is a Pain in the Neck
Frankenstein Moved in on the Fourth Floor
Wolfman Sam

The Black Cat Club • Saunders
#1 The Ghost Who Ate Chocolate
#2 The Haunted Skateboard
#3 The Curse of the Cat Mummy
#4 The Ghost of Spirit Lake
#5 The Revenge of the Pirate Ghost
#6 The Phantom Pen Pal

The Adam Joshua Capers • Smith
#1 The Monster in the Third Dresser Drawer
#2 The Kid Next Door
#3 Super-Kid!
#4 The Show-and-Tell War
#5 The Halloween Monster
#6 George Takes a Bow-Wow!
#7 Turkey Trouble
#8 The Christmas Ghost
#9 Nelson in Love
#10 Serious Science
#11 The Baby Blues

The Weebie Zone • Spinner/Weiss
#1 Gerbilitis
#2 Sing, Elvis, Sing!
#3 Born to Be Wild
#4 Bright Lights, Little Gerbil